MAGNIFICENT MAGICAL BEASTS

Inside Their Secret World

SIMON HOLLAND

illustrated by

GARY BLYTHE • DAVID DEMARET • NELSON EVERGREEN • JOHN HOWE
MIKE LOVE • KEV WALKER • HELEN WARD • DAVID WYATT

BLOOMSBURY
NEW YORK LONDON OXFORD NEW DELHI SYDNEY

Contents

A World of Magical Beasts

**W**elcome to an enchanted world of strange and magical beasts. For many thousands of years, people have told stories about creatures that lurk in mysterious places that are beyond human control, such as caves, mountains, rivers, lakes, the air, and the ocean. Legends say that supernatural beings can weave their magic in all these places. Watch out for an elf who might bring bad fortune, give you nightmares, or make food go bad, or an angry giant who carves out valleys and scatters mountains across the land. Or perhaps you might meet a dragon or a magical serpent who can conjure rain, sleet, snow, and storms from the air.

Many of the exotic beasts you'll meet in this book have human features, or are part human and part animal. Some of them are a medley of different animal parts. There is the terrifying basilisk, part serpent and part cockerel; the noble griffin, part lion, part eagle; and the mighty centaur, half man, half horse. There are alluring selkies, beautiful creatures who switch from human to seal, and mysterious werewolves, who shift their shape from human to wolf and back again. Prepare to be enchanted, frightened, and amazed, all at the same time, when you dare to enter this spellbinding realm.

"Glorious phoenix,"
cried the Sun [god].
"You shall be my bird
and live forever!"

Phoenix

Fantastically beautiful birds often appear in mythological stories connected to ideas of death, rebirth, and immortality. The phoenix is one such bird from the Middle East. Every five or six centuries, the bird senses it is time to die, and it builds a "funeral nest" out of sweet-smelling sticks and herbs from Arabian spice groves. The phoenix then lies down to rest and sings an enchanting song as the sun rises and sets fire to the nest. Both the bird and the nest are turned to ashes—but a seed of life remains . . .

A tiny worm crawls from the ashes and grows into a new young phoenix. This chick collects the ashes into an egg made from myrrh, a gumlike material that comes from trees. According to some versions of the legend, the phoenix takes to the sky—surrounded by other birds—and carries the egg to Heliopolis, the Egyptian City of the Sun. Here, the egg is delivered to priests at a temple, where the ashes may be buried. The bird is now free to return to Arabia and begin its new life.

The immortal phoenix is a powerful symbol of hope—the triumph of new life over death.

The true home of the phoenix is Paradise. In our world, only one such bird can live at any one time.

In ancient Egyptian mythology, the phoenix is a female firebird with dazzling red-and-gold feathers that lives for either 500 or 1,461 years. This bird is sometimes pictured as a heron or a flamingo-like bird from East Africa and can regenerate itself if wounded by an enemy.

In ancient Greek and Roman legends, the bird looks more like a peacock or an eagle. Most of the phoenix stories feature a sun god riding across the sky in a horse-drawn chariot who stops to listen to the bird's haunting song.

5

Giants

Giants are all around us in the worlds of magic and mythology. They often have a close connection with nature. In some cultures, stories are told of giants who build mountains or become parts of the living landscape. In Scandinavia, frost giants created the highlands and carved out the valleys in between them. Russian giants, known as Asilky, dug out huge spaces for rivers and lakes and piled up the earth and rocks into mountains.

These giants of folklore have battles that make the earth shake. Once, an Irish giant called Finn McCool wanted to pick a fight with his enemy, a Scottish giant named Benandonner. Finn shaped the coastline by picking up great chunks of the landscape and hurling them into the sea. His aim was to form a pathway so that he could march over to the other giant and fight. Finn retreated when he saw how massive his opponent was. Benandonner came out looking for Finn, but Finn's wife saved the day by playing tricks on Benandonner so that he ran back home. The Scottish giant then tore up the causeway, hurling the rocks into the sea so that Finn couldn't follow him home.

It is said that the Giant's Causeway, a natural stone formation in Northern Ireland, is what's left of the path built and then torn up by giants.

The giant Finn McCool (or Fionn mac Cumhaill) calls out to his enemy across the water, challenging him to fight.

Benandonner was so huge that his advance across the Causeway made the earth tremble and Finn shake with fear.

Fearsome Giants

Giants are powerful forces of nature. They do battle with gods by hurling immense pieces of the landscape at them, or cause great alarm to human beings by fighting amongst themselves. Huge rocks or standing stones are sometimes said to be the left-overs of a skirmish between two giants, who argued and threw boulders at each other. Other stories tell of giants who shape or turn into parts of the natural world—or who use the winter weather to travel from place to place while altering their physical shape.

CYCLOPES

The one-eyed Cyclopes of Greek myths were skilled blacksmiths who forged weapons the gods used in their war against other giants, the Titans.

ASILKY

The Asilky, mighty giants from Russia, formed the mountains, rivers, and lakes of the earth. They had to be destroyed when, having become too proud, they rose up against God.

WINDIGOS

In southern Canada, the Algonquin people tell stories of windigos, cannibal ice giants that can take the forms of a tree-sized man or a giant timber wolf. They use blizzards and winds to travel without being seen so that they can harm humans.

Harpies

These vengeful spirits may once have been beautiful women, but they have transformed into ugly, twisted monsters of the sky. Harpies have the face and body of a woman, but also the wings and talons of a ferocious, vulture-like bird—and one of the most frightening things about them is that nobody truly knows how many of them exist.

Harpies are the most dangerous beings of the Underworld in ancient Greek mythology, and their robber-like behavior is what earns them their name—the word "harpy" comes from a Greek word that means "snatcher." They are sometimes depicted as birds of prey with the faces of women, swooping down to grab people or torment them by stealing their food and possessions. Arriving in storms and whirlwinds, they take what they came for and leave behind a foul smell of decay. This is why they were often seen as symbols of death and destruction in ancient Greek society.

Harpies are lovely-haired creatures, but everything else about them is dirty, foul, and terrifying.

*"Here the repellent harpies make their nests . . .
They have broad wings, a human neck and face,
Clawed feet and swollen, feathered bellies; they caw
Their lamentations in the eerie trees."*

DANTE, *INFERNO*

There are harpies at large in the natural world today. A bird of prey from the tropical forests of Central and South America behaves just like these predatory creatures, which is why it is called the harpy eagle. This bird is large enough to prey on big, heavy mammals such as sloths and monkeys. When it's ready to strike, it drops from the sky, extends its powerful claws, and snatches its victim from the treetops, reminding us of those frightful harpies that emerge from the wind!

11

Unicorns

Unicorns often remind us of fantasy stories or the romantic legends of medieval times, but they actually come from much earlier tales told by travelers to India as long ago as the 4th century BCE. These Indian unicorns had white bodies, purple heads, and deep blue eyes, as well as single horns of about twenty inches long. In European tales of the 12th century, unicorns appear as white, wild, horselike beasts—also with a single spiral horn—that are very difficult to catch and tame.

A Western unicorn is known for its loud, wild, untamed bellowing.

UNICORN LORE

If a lord or ruler feared he might be poisoned by one of his enemies, he might have a special goblet crafted for him, made from the horn of a unicorn. The horn was supposed to neutralize any poison added to the cup—but in fact, the horn usually came from a narwhal (a kind of whale with a long tusk).

In the Western stories, a unicorn can only be tamed by a young girl or woman who is able to coax the animal into resting its head in her lap. The unicorn then settles and falls asleep. This is the moment when greedy hunters might try to cut the precious horn from the animal's head. Like the claws of the Indian griffin, a unicorn's horn has magical, healing powers. It can detect poison in any liquid, such as water, and then purify it to make it safe.

The unicorn is known as the Kirin in Japan, and as the Ki Lin (or Ch'i Lin) in China. In the writings of ancient China, the Ki Lin has a single horn and the hooves of a horse, but the body of a deer. The Japanese Kirin is similar to the Ki Lin, but its body is covered in scales. These Eastern unicorns are much tamer and more peaceful than their Western cousins. The Ki Lin is so gentle that it always treads carefully, in case it should harm any insects or small creatures living underfoot.

Western unicorns (right) are visions of sleekness and elegance, but they are also fierce and untamed. Eastern unicorns (left) are gentle, tame, and peaceful.

13

Centaurs

ythology is a place where we can meet all kinds of beings, from humanlike spirits to hybrids formed from two or more different animals. Centaurs combine the physical strength and agility of horses with the mental capacity of humans. Chiron was the most famous and most skillful of these creatures—an immortal being and master of the healing arts who was also much gentler than other centaurs. In fact, Chiron became so knowledgeable that he was chosen as a teacher for Greek heroes and the sons of gods.

One day, Chiron was accidently wounded by a poisoned arrow. Although he could have lived forever, he decided to give away his immortality so that he wouldn't have to live on in pain. Zeus, the king of the Olympian gods, then created an image of Chiron in the night sky, which we can see as the constellation called Sagittarius, so that he could be remembered by both gods and mortals.

Different stories say different things about how the centaurs came to be half man, half horse. Some suggest the centaurs are a product of a union between a giant and a race of horses, while others say that the centaurs were once giants, called Titans, who fought the gods. The Titans were defeated and given the lower bodies of horses as a punishment for their rebellion.

PART MAN, PART BEAST
Other hybrid creatures include the bull-headed Minotaur that haunted the labyrinth of King Minos, in Crete. Also from Greek mythology are the fauns and satyrs. Satyrs appear either as a man with a horse's ears and tail or as a man with a goat's ears, legs, tail, and horns. Fauns are part man, part goat.

Centaurs such as Chiron combine the physical prowess of a horse with the intelligence of a human being.

Spirits of the forest and animal kingdom come together in the form of a faun. Fauns are not always trustworthy. It is hard to know if they are going to help you or deceive you.

15

Basilisks

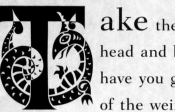ake the tail of a serpent, add the head and body of a cockerel, and what have you got? Answer: a basilisk, one of the weirdest and most dangerous beasts in the whole of mythology. In Greek, its name means "little king." This is because, in its earliest form, a basilisk was a small snake with a kingly, crown-shaped crest on its head. In later legends from the Middle Ages, basilisks emerged from eggs that had been laid by a cockerel—sometimes on a mound of dung—and kept warm by a snake or toad until they hatched.

There are many different ways in which a basilisk can kill: it can scorch things with its fiery breath, spit venom, or kill with its touch, its stench, or even its evil stare. In short, it's not a good idea to go anywhere near it! This fearsome beast can also pollute water for hundreds of years by drinking from a pool or well. Only three things can destroy a basilisk: seeing its own stare reflected in a mirror or pond, a cockerel crowing, or smelling its greatest enemy, the weasel.

This beast can kill with a roar
or a hiss, with its stench, or
even with a single look.

Some basilisks have sharp talons and teeth, while others have dragon-like wings or a long, snakelike tail.

Anyone who sees the eyes of a basilisk serpent dies immediately. It is no more than twelve inches long and has white markings on its head that look like a diadem. Unlike other snakes, which flee its hiss, it moves forward with its middle raised high. Its touch and even its breath scorch grass, kill bushes, and burst rocks. Its poison is so deadly that once when a man on a horse speared a basilisk, the venom traveled up the spear and killed not only the man but also the horse.

BASED ON PLINY THE ELDER'S
NATURAL HISTORY (1ST CENTURY CE)

Trolls

Trolls are among the many supernatural beings that come to us from Old Norse mythology. Some of them may be the same as (or related to) the Jötnar, cruel giants who were enemies of the gods. Trolls are gigantic, smelly, hideous, evil-minded beings, inhumanly strong and foul-tempered. They live deep inside mountains, caves, and burrows, where they hide away from sunlight during the day.

Like people, these beasts may live together in small family groups. However, they don't seem to enjoy mixing with humans and would never go out of their way to be helpful to them! By night, they wander out to hide in the shadows and hunt their prey, which might include human beings. If a person ever comes across a troll, a good thing to do is run—and keep on running—until sunrise, or until the troll is far away from its home. When the sun comes up, the troll will be doomed: sunlight turns all trolls to stone.

In later Scandinavian folktales, trolls have evolved into beings that are less grotesque and a little more like "real" people. But beware—these trolls are still considered to be highly dangerous, and their remote homes (far from human towns and villages) should never be approached.

Take another look at the rocks, hills, and mountains you are stepping over—they could be trolls that have turned to stone.

They call me a troll,
moon of the earth-Hrungnir,
wealth-sucker of the giant,
destroyer of the storm-sun,
beloved follower of the seeress,
guardian of the "nafjord,"
swallower of the wheel of heaven.
What's a troll if not that?
FROM OLD NORSE *SKÁLDSKAPARMÁL*,
TRANSLATED BY JOHN LINDOW

Trolls vary in their appearance.
They may look ugly, slow, docile,
humanlike, or like a part of
the landscape—but they should
always be avoided.

Merpeople

The tales of seagoing nations sometimes tell of "halfway" people, whose human forms are blended with the bodies of sea ceatures. Fishing people in Greenland describe the hideous Margyr, which has the characteristics of a walrus, while the First Nation tribes of Canada have swapped stories about half-fish people who create sea storms when they are angry.

Across the ocean, in Japan, there is the ningyo, a fish with the head of a human and the mouth of a monkey. Ningyos are bringers of storms and bad luck—so if fishermen catch them, they have to remember to throw them back into the sea.

Selkies are "seal-women" who, every ninth night, shed their skin in order to come ashore and live as real women. They sometimes have relationships with human men, but usually they feel a powerful urge to return to the ocean.

SIRENS

The sirens of ancient Greek stories are often confused with mermaids. The sirens sang songs that attracted sailors to their island, where they would meet their doom.

Melusine was a similar character from French and German folklore. She appeared to be a human woman, but once a week, in the privacy of her bath and away from prying eyes, she would secretly grow wings and a serpent's tail.

Then, of course, there are mermaids—beautiful women from the waist upward, who have the tail of a fish. Mermaids are usually described as vain creatures with beautiful singing voices who love to tend their lustrous hair.

Men are often bewitched by the beauty of the selkies and end up heartbroken when they return to the sea.

The ocean is a dark and frightening place for humans to visit. It's no wonder we see so many beasts in the water.

Dragons

Stories of serpents and dragons come from all over the world. In the West, dragons tend to be violent, destructive creatures that breathe fire and deliver floods to the land. They often need to be hunted down and killed by brave knights and warriors in order for peace and prosperity to return. Dragons are sometimes associated with evil or the devil—as in the legend of Saint Michael, who had to fight a dragon and expel it from the heavenly kingdom.

Saint George was another famous dragon-slayer, from the Middle East, who encountered a dragon that made its home in a lake near a town in Libya. Every time the townspeople wanted to draw water from the home of the dragon, the beast would demand the sacrifice of a young girl from the town. In some versions of his legend, Saint George arrived to find the daughter of a king, who had been tied up and left for the dragon to eat. He then rescued the princess by either killing or wounding the dragon.

Earthly fire and dragon fire are two opposing forces in Western mythology. When doused with water, earthly fire may be extinguished, while dragon fire continues to burn. However, dragon fire can be put out by earthly fire.

UNDERWATER KING

Chinese tales feature rain-bringing dragons that live at the bottom of pools, springs, and lakes.

Guide to Dragons

Eastern dragons are very different from Western dragons. They have feet with claws attached to a serpent-like body, but they do not have wings. Instead, they fly using a more magical form of energy. Dragons of the East lay eggs, which take around 3,000 years to hatch. However, once a newborn dragon has broken free of its egg, it takes just minutes to expand from a tiny, snakelike being into its majestic, full-grown form.

RAIN BEARER

In a time of drought, these Buddhist monks are holding a ceremony to summon up the rain dragon Sui-Riu, the Japanese "dragon king," so that he may bring back the rains.

JEWEL GUARDIAN

In Malaysia, a dragon jealously guards a valuable jewel at the summit of Mount Kinabalu. He emerges from his hiding place on moonlit nights.

MYSTERIOUS GIANT SERPENT

Most Korean dragons begin life as an imugi, a gigantic serpent that may—after many years—mature into a fully formed dragon.

In Eastern mythology,

dragons are not terrible, but powerful and magnificent. In China and Vietnam, for example, they are symbols of life, happiness, growth, and fertility. They are the weather-lords who guard the rivers and lakes and bring rain to the land. They battle each other in the sky to create thunderous storms or fight in the water to cause floods. In Chinese legends, dragons sleep at the bottoms of pools in the winter, then rise up in the spring and turn into rain clouds. Similarly, in Japanese mythology, people try to wake up the water dragons in times of drought, angering the creatures and causing them to leap up into the sky and make rain showers.

Werewolves

Terrifying werewolves have appeared in stories for many centuries—but where did the creature originally come from? One of the earliest man-wolf tales is that of Lycaon, a king of Arcadia. The Greek god Zeus visited the king disguised as a humble traveler. Lycaon tested Zeus by serving him a meal made from the flesh of Nyctimus, one of Lycaon's fifty sons. This enraged Zeus, who then transformed the king into a wolf. Today, we still use the word "lycanthropy" to mean the magical transformation of a person into a wolflike being.

The name werewolf comes from two Old English words—"wer" (man) and "wulf" (wolf)—fused together to make "werewulf" (man-wolf). The werewolves of later folktales are shape-shifters that turn into their wolflike form at certain times or under particular circumstances. Some European stories tell of wolf people who can transform themselves deliberately, more or less when they feel like it. They do so by taking off their clothes and putting on a special belt or strap made from wolfskin, by rubbing their body with a magical ointment, or through some other kind of natural trickery.

*Even a man
who is pure in heart
And says his prayers by night
May become a wolf
When the wolfbane blooms
And the autumn moon is bright.*
CURT SIODMAK, *THE WOLF MAN*

In other stories, somebody might turn into an animal (such as a wolf) by drinking rainwater from the footprint of that animal, or by sleeping outdoors at night on a specific day of the week, with a full moon shining directly down into their face. Other people simply disappear from their home or village for certain days each week while they spend time living in the form of a wolf.

In 21st-century stories, people who become werewolves often lose all control over their natural instincts—they howl at the moon, tear around the countryside on all fours, attack humans, and even dig up freshly buried bodies to get at their flesh. Victims of these creatures may also become werewolves if they are bitten.

In the lands of European folklore, there are people who live many days of their lives in the form of a wolf or wolf-person.

How to Outwit a Werewolf

**W**erewolves can be incredibly strong, fast, and cruel—so is there any surefire way of overcoming them? To get the better of a werewolf you'll need to know all about how they change from person to wolf and back again, and how to find one, before you can even think of outwitting it.

A full moon is sometimes the cause of the transformation from person into beast. In many folktales, a person can transform himself or herself into a werewolf by using a magic "wolf strap." This gives the werewolf control over when he changes and changes back. In one story from Germany, a little boy would put on the wolf strap whenever his family was away from home. He would become a werewolf and frighten and chase his friends.

Werewolves are not easy to find. They are secretive and mischievous, and when they get found out they normally escape and move to the next town, and the next, and the next. But sometimes, preventing a werewolf from changing back into a human will trap it.

In the 12th-century French tale of Baron Bisclavret, each week, for three whole days, the baron would turn into a wolf. He tried to keep this a secret by hiding each time the wolf form came upon him. Eventually, though, he admitted to his wife that he was a werewolf. He told her that he had to hide his clothing in a safe place each week so that he could dress as himself again and return to human form.

As a wolf, Baron Bisclavret was mainly gentle. He only became vicious in the moment of revenge.

KILLING A WERE-BEAST

In some folktales, a werewolf can be wounded or destroyed using silver. A weapon forged from this precious metal may be used, although sometimes it needs to have been blessed by a priest. Silver bullets (either blessed or unblessed) can also kill or injure werewolves.

SHAPE-SHIFTERS

Shape-shifters are beings that can turn themselves into another form. They may shift into the shape of an animal, shrink to become tiny, or swell up to a gigantic size. Shape-shifters sometimes use their magic to trick people or escape from the scene of a crime.

Disgusted by his revelation, the baron's wife instructed a knight to find and steal Bisclavret's clothes. Without his human outfit, the baron became fixed in his wolf form and could not return to his home. Later, however, the werewolf got his revenge. The gentle beast was adopted by the king and went to live at his court. One day, the baroness visited the king's court and Bisclavret immediately recognized his former wife. He attacked her and bit off her nose.

TELLTALE WOUNDS

In some tales, a dangerous, out-of-control werewolf may be hunted and struck, but may survive and escape. However, its wound prevents it from transforming back into its wolf form. A human you find limping around or hiding a suspicious wound may be the injured wolf!

The Chimera

This creature comes from a ghastly family, so it's no wonder that she's such a terrible beast to behold. Her father is an ancient Greek fire-breathing giant called Typhon, while her mother is a part-woman, part-serpent named Echidna, the goddess of illness and disease. The Chimera's own body has the legs and foreparts of a lion, an extra head (that of a goat) and a dragon-like tail that ends with the head of a snake. So, that's three heads in all—just like her brother, Cerberus, the three-headed hound who guards the gates of the Greek underworld (see pages 34–35).

The Chimera made her home on a mountain in Lycia. Using the highlands as her lair, she terrorized the people of the surrounding kingdom with her incredible speed and breath of fire. This misery went on for many years, until King Iobates of Lycia decided to give a series of tasks to a local hero called Prince Bellerophon (see pages 40–41). The first of these heroic challenges was to destroy the Chimera.

The Chimera is a child of monsters. She comes from one of the most abominable families in mythology.

As with many beasts

from mythology, the Chimera appears in different forms when featured in stories or depicted in works of art. The beast has come to represent death and destruction, but is also connected with natural disasters such as storms and shipwrecks. The fiery eruptions of volcanoes, too, are sometimes compared with the flaming breath of the horrible Chimera.

"...A thing of immortal make, not human, lion-fronted and snake behind, a goat in the middle, and snorting out the breath of the terrible flame of bright fire..."
HOMER, *THE ILIAD*, BOOK SIX, TRANSLATED BY RICHMOND LATTIMORE

Sphinxes

These very mysterious creatures first appeared in the mythology of ancient Egypt and the Middle East before being taken into the culture of the ancient Greeks. In the Egyptian tradition, sphinxes have lionlike bodies and the head of a human, hawk, or ram—whereas Greek sphinxes have the wings of an eagle and the head of a woman on the body of a lion. The most famous sphinx from Greek mythology is the offspring of Typhon and Echidna, as is the three-headed Chimera.

In the Greek legends, the gods were offended by the people of Thebes, a city in ancient Greece, so they sent the Sphinx to punish them. She did this by confronting Theban travelers and asking them a challenging riddle:

What goes on four feet, on two feet, and three— but the more feet it goes on, the weaker it be?

Nobody ever wanted to encounter the Sphinx, because she strangled and ate any passersby who were unable to solve the puzzle . . . until, one day, a man named Oedipus came up with the answer. He correctly worked out that the Sphinx was describing a human being: a person crawls on all fours as a baby, gets up on two feet as a child and an adult, and then needs a third leg— a walking stick—as a support in old age.

Upon hearing the correct answer, the Sphinx was thrown into a rage and dashed herself against the rocks, killing herself in an instant. As a reward for freeing the land from the monster, Oedipus was made king of Thebes.

OTHER SPHINXES

In other cultures, "human-beast" sphinxes can serve as trusted guardians and protectors. The Great Sphinx of Giza, in Egypt, still stands beside the pyramid tombs of the pharaohs Khufu, Khafra, and Menkaura. Indian sphinxes, known as *purushamrigas*, are protectors of temples and the people who come to worship in them.

Passing travelers go in fear of the Sphinx. Should she swoop down and challenge them, they may not live to tell the tale.

Cerberus

In many mythologies, doorways and gateways are seen as important places that need to be protected by gods, spirits, or other beings. The ancient Romans, for example, had several gods that looked after the doors of a house: Janus was the god of doorways and beginnings, with two heads for looking both ways, while Limentius was the god of the threshold (the part of an entrance that you step over). If everyday doorways are important, a doorway from one world to another is even more special and powerful. Such a doorway may have fearsome or awe-inspiring beasts as "guardians of the watch" living at its gates, to stop people from passing in and out.

Cerberus, a three-headed hound, is one such guardian. His Greek name, Kerberos, may mean "demon of the pit"—for he is the Hound of Hades, lord of the Underworld, and gatekeeper of the Underworld in Greek mythology.

As well as three heads, Cerberus also has a dragon's tail—and is sometimes described as having a mane of serpents growing out of his back.

Cerberus's many heads allow him to keep

watch in several directions at once. When dead people reach the entrance
to the Underworld, they are greeted by the watchdog. He allows them in
but never lets them out again. Usually, the only way to calm this terrifying
hound is by bringing him honey cakes to eat—but you have to remember
to bring one for each head! Feeding him his favorite food will keep his
awesome jaws occupied while you pass from one world to the next.

Fearsome Gatekeepers

Cerberus is not the only beast to guard the entrance to a land of the dead. There are other animal-like gatekeepers in myths and legends. Each has an important role to play when they meet those on their path into the next world.

GARMR

This enormous hound has four eyes, and its jaws and body are dripping with the blood of the dead. It guards the gates of Helheim, the land of the dead in Norse mythology. Garmr is the hound of Hel, the Norse goddess of Helheim—just as Cerberus is the hound of Hades, the Greek god of the dead.

YAMA'S HOUNDS

In Indian (Hindu) writings, the "next world" of the dead is controlled by the god Yama, thought to be the first being ever to die. Yama has two four-eyed hounds named Shyama the Black and Sabala the Spotted. Frightful but also helpful, these creatures seek out the dead and lead them into Yama's "kingdom of light."

HERACLES AND CERBERUS

Heracles is a hero of Greek mythology who was ordered to carry out Twelve Labors (tasks) as a punishment for crimes he had committed. The twelfth of these tasks was to drag Cerberus out from the Underworld and into the daylight.

AMMUT

Ancient Egyptian mythology is famous for its depictions of the underworld, which is guarded by a goddess called Ammut (or Ammit). Ammut has the head of a crocodile, the forelimbs of a lion and the rear end of a hippo. The goddess sits next to the scales when the heart of a dead person is weighed: if the heart is heavier than a feather, Ammut will eat the heart and its owner will be refused entry into the underworld.

Griffins

The griffin, or gryphon, is a magnificent beast with the body and hind legs of a lion, a feathered back, and the head, beak, wings, and claws of an eagle. In some stories, it also has a serpent's tail. High up in the mountains of India, it digs for gold and uses the precious metal to forge its nest.

Griffins are highly protective of their young. They collect a gem called agate, which acts as a medicine to keep their babies from getting sick. Because their nests are full of glittering treasure, people often try to steal from them—but if a griffin catches any thieves in the act, it will kill them and feed their remains to its hungry offspring. This is why these beasts are greatly feared. Yet, a griffin's favorite food is a live horse.

STRANGE HYBRID

If a griffin mates with a horse, a "hippogriff" will be born. But this creature is very rare, given that griffins despise horses and love to eat them!

Because of how rare and ferocious these creatures are, the body parts of griffins are highly prized by the medieval kings and noblemen of fairy tales. People boast of drinking from the hollowed-out claws of a griffin, and young heroes may be set the task of stealing from the animal or taking a feather from its back or tail.

The claws of the griffin are highly prized. By changing color, they warn that poison is nearby.

Pegasus

AS the story goes, the magical winged horse Pegasus sprang into being when the terrifying, snake-headed Medusa was slain. Medusa was the ghastly Gorgon from Greek mythology, who turned all who saw her to stone. One fateful day, she was slain by the hero Perseus, and when he cut off her head, her blood gushed forth—and a winged horse sprang from the blood. That horse was named Pegasus. Pegasus flew to Mount Helicon, the home of the Muses, the nine goddesses of the arts and sciences, who cared for him.

It was wonderful indeed that such a gentle, graceful creature could spring from the blood of a Gorgon.

A hero called Bellerophon desired to catch, tame, and ride this special horse, but was unable to do so until the goddess Athena granted him a magical golden bridle. Later, Bellerophon was set the task of vanquishing the terrible Chimera (see pages 30–31). Because he now had Pegasus under his control, he was able to ride the horse high into the sky and fire his arrows down on the Chimera—from a safe distance—and destroy it.

Having completed this difficult task, Bellerophon became arrogant and tried to ride Pegasus to Mount Olympus, the home of the gods, where no mortal was meant to go. Angered by this, the gods sent a gadfly to sting Pegasus, causing the horse to throw off his rider, who fell back down to the ground. Pegasus was welcomed into the "heavenly stables" in the sky, where he became a dazzling constellation (a pattern of stars).

Pegasus, the seventh largest constellation, can be seen in the skies of the northern hemisphere.

INSPIRING HORSE

Wherever Pegasus struck a hoof on the ground, a fountain sprang up. To please the Muses, he struck a hoof on the ground of Mount Helicon and conjured up the "spring of inspiration" known as Hippocrene.

Elves

Human communities have been telling stories about elves and fairies for more than 2,000 years. Some elves are tiny, others very tall. They appear in many different forms, but can be grouped together as the Little People who live in the countryside, where the worlds of people and fairies sometimes come together. In different cultures, these creatures have very different personalities. Some of them are useful and helpful to humans, while others can be spiteful or downright mischievous if they are not treated with respect.

Look closely and you might see kobolds leaving their day's work, an empty fairy ring, and nasty elves pestering people as they walk to market.

The Fynoderee, from the Isle of Man, is a small, shaggy creature who helps farmers gather in the crops at harvest time—unless they offend him! The kobolds of German folklore are similar: if they're in a good mood, these goblin-like creatures will leave their homes to come and help humans with household chores or even work in the mines. But if they feel like it, they might play a nasty trick on the people of the house—just like the Celtic boggarts, who love to bang pots and pans together, keeping everyone awake!

Playful spirits of the countryside follow our every step, in the world of European folklore.

Boggarts are keeping people awake with their boisterous tricks.

In Germany, if you suffer from alpdrücken, or "elf-pressure," it means you're having terrible nightmares. The word comes from tales in which troublesome elves sit on people's chests at night. If farmers are not careful, elves will steal their cows, milk, bread—and even their babies.

Elves can make themselves disappear, too. They make farming people think they are walking toward a "fairy market," only for the market to disappear as the humans get close—but the farmers can feel little people bumping into them, as if they're walking through a real market.

Elvish Spells and Tricks

Elves and fairies sometimes create connections with the human world. But beware if you're unlucky enough to meet a mischievous elf! Watch out for these common tricks and spells . . .

ELFIN MISCHIEF

While some elves are helpful to countryfolk, others delight in playing tricks. They might steal cows, milk, and bread from farmers—or make their milk and cream curdle (go lumpy).

FAIRY RING

Beautiful elvish women will sometimes cast spells over the young, human men to whom they are attracted. They use their power to lure them into a "fairy ring," from which the men then struggle to escape. These elves also like to steal human babies, replacing them with an elf-child known as a "changeling."

HARVEST HELP

The Fynoderee, from the Isle of Man, is a goblin who helps with farm work at harvest time—but he'll leave you to do all the work if you get on his nerves!

ELF-NIGHTMARES

Some elves will sit on your chest at night to give you alpdrücken (or "elf-pressure"), which leads to terrible nightmares.

ELF-HORSES

Lutins are French hobgoblins that can turn themselves into horses and spiders. As horses, they try and get people to mount and ride them, so that they can throw them into a muddy ditch . . . just for fun!

ELF-ENTANGLEMENT

If you wake up in the morning with tangled hair, it might be that playful elves have given you "elf-locks."

ENDLESS ELVES

All of these beings are types of elves and fairies:

bogeymen, bogglemen, bodachs, brownies, bubaks, bugaboos, bugbears, goblins, leprechauns, pixies, sprites

Magical Words

agate a semiprecious gemstone, often with bright bands of color running through it

Algonquin native North American people, most of whom live in Quebec, in eastern Canada

Athena the ancient Greek goddess of wisdom and military victory

boggart a household spirit— sometimes helpful, sometimes mischievous or nasty

changeling when elves steal an infant from its parents, they secretly put a changeling (an elf-child) in its place

constellation a group of stars that forms a pattern we can recognize and give a name to

diadem a type of jeweled royal crown

fertility of land: the ability to support plentiful crops; or of animals or plants: the ability to have offspring or babies

gadfly a type of biting, stinging fly that especially annoys horses

First Nations the native people of Canada

Hades ruler of the Underworld, or land of the dead, in Greek mythology

hybrid the offspring (young) of two different types of plant or animal

immortal everlasting, never-dying; gods and goddesses are described as immortal, whereas humans are mortal

knight a soldier from the Middle Ages who fought on horseback and served a lord

Minotaur a monster from Greek legends that is half man, half bull

Mount Olympus the home of the 12 major gods of ancient Greek mythology

myrrh a resin obtained from certain trees, which has a pleasant smell

Norse a word used to refer to things from medieval Norwegian language and culture, or from Scandinavia in general

riddle a question, statement, or poem that contains a hidden meaning; intelligence or logic is needed to discover the answer

sacrifice something that is offered to a god or goddess in return for his or her good favor; this might include a human or animal sacrifice

Scandinavia the region of northwest Europe that contains the countries of Norway, Sweden, Denmark, Finland, Iceland, and the Faroe Islands

sirens three enchanting creatures, half woman and half bird, from Greek mythology; the sirens cast spells over sailors with their bewitching singing

Thebes a city in central Greece, an important setting for many ancient Greek legends

Titans a race of gods that existed before the 12 Olympian gods in ancient Greek mythology

Underworld in many mythologies, including ancient Egyptian, Greek, and Roman, the place where souls go after death

Zeus the supreme god in ancient Greek mythology, god of the sky and storms and protector and ruler of humankind

First published in Great Britain in October 2016 by Bloomsbury Publishing Plc
Published in the United States of America in October 2016 by Bloomsbury Children's Books
www.bloomsbury.com

Bloomsbury is a registered trademark of Bloomsbury Publishing Plc

For information about permission to reproduce selections from this book, write to
Permissions, Bloomsbury Children's Books, 1385 Broadway, New York, New York 10018
Bloomsbury books may be purchased for business or promotional use. For information on
bulk purchases please contact Macmillan Corporate and Premium Sales Department at
specialmarkets@macmillan.com

Library of Congress Cataloging-in-Publication Data
available upon request
ISBN 978-1-68119-430-1 (hardcover)

Printed and bound in Italy by L.E.G.O. Spa, Vicenza
2 4 6 8 10 9 7 5 3 1

All papers used by Bloomsbury Publishing, Inc., are natural, recyclable products
made from wood grown in well-managed forests. The manufacturing processes
conform to the environmental regulations of the country of origin.